To Archie and Haydn

Copyright © 2016 by Richard Collingridge
All rights reserved. Published by Scholastic Inc., *Publishers since 1920*, by arrangement with David Fickling Books, Oxford, England. SCHOLASTIC and associated logos are trademarks and/or registered trademarks of Scholastic Inc. DAVID FICKLING BOOKS and associated logos are trademarks and/or registered trademarks of David Fickling Books.

First published in the United Kingdom by David Fickling Books,
31 Beaumont Street, Oxford OX1 2NP.
www.davidficklingbooks.com

Library of Congress Cataloging-in-Publication Data Available

ISBN 978-0-545-83321-9

10 9 8 7 6 5 4 3 2 1   16 17 18 19 20

Warning: This book will make you ROAR!

Printed in China   137
First edition, March 2016
Book design by Ness Wood

LIONHEART

RICHARD COLLINGRIDGE

David Fickling Books

Scholastic Inc. • New York

"There can't be.
There can't be.
There's no such thing
as monsters."

But what was that sound?

Richard hugged his
Lionheart tightly.

Something was there
and Richard was scared.

So he ran . . .

He ran and he ran,
through the streets
and over the hills,
through the forest
and into the fields.

But he was being chased . . .

All around him the grass grew thick, and turned into sticks,
and the sticks grew tall, and turned into trees,

but still he was being chased . . .

so Richard kept running.

Until he ran into

a magical jungle . . .

. . . where there were
animals all around.

Some big, some small,
some thin, some tall,
some mean, some hairy,
some fat, some scary.

But Richard couldn't stay to look.

The monster was coming . . .

so Richard kept running.

He ran and he ran

until . . .

He ran into something . . .

or some*one*!

It was Lionheart!
But he wasn't a toy anymore.

"Come with me!"
his Lionheart said.
And Richard went.

Away from the monster.
Away from his fears.

Together they jumped over the pointing rocks

and went under the falling water.

They traveled deep, deep,
deep into the Lost City,
where Richard played
with the animals.

And he was having
so much fun that
he forgot the monster.

He forgot he was scared.

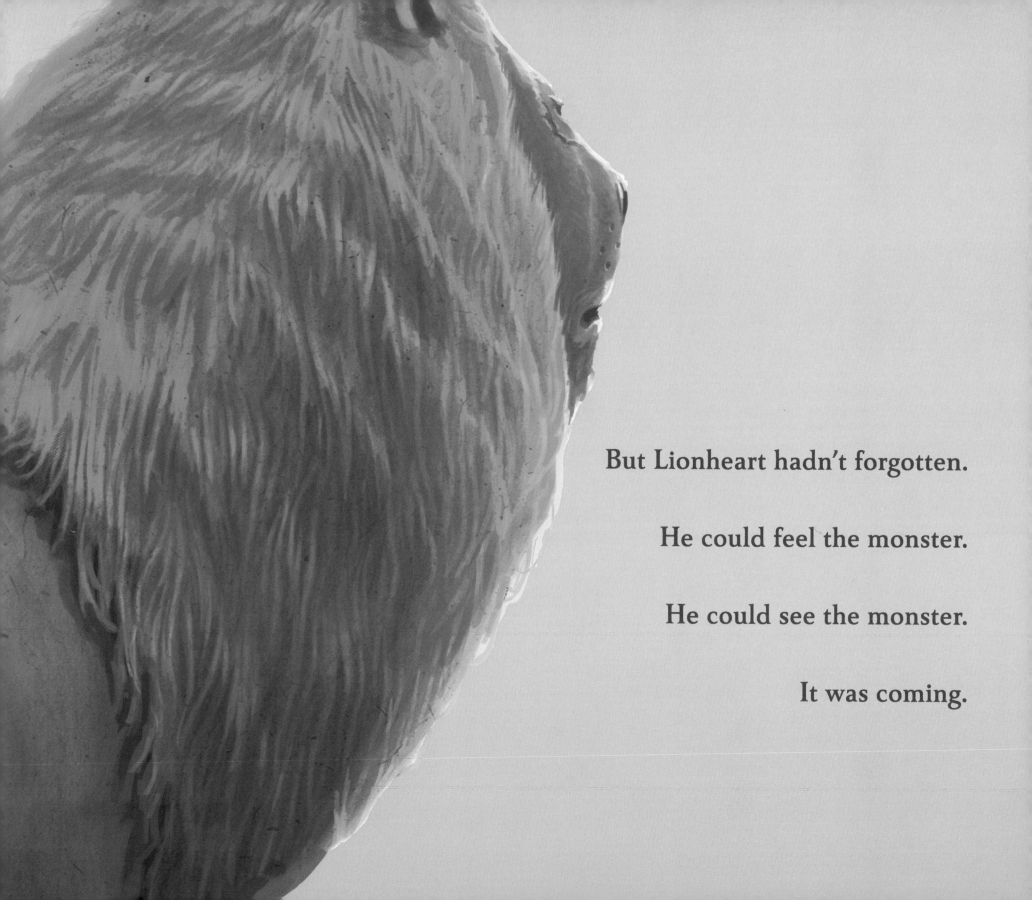

But Lionheart hadn't forgotten.

He could feel the monster.

He could see the monster.

It was coming.

The animals saw it too, and they were scared.

Then Richard saw it!

But when Richard
looked at Lionheart
he knew what
to do. He knew
how to be brave —
his Lionheart
had shown him.

So together they
took a deep breath
and started to . . .

ROAR!

They roared SO loudly that
the monster and all of
Richard's fears

were blown away
once and for all!

And Richard wasn't afraid of monsters anymore.